Dear Parents,

*Psalty in the Soviet Circus* shows the importance of
memorizing Scripture. There are difficult times in
everyone's life when certain Scripture verses can become
especially meaningful. If we hide God's Word in our hearts
it can be remembered when we need it. In this book Psalty
the Singing Songbook is comforted by the verse "I will
never leave you [or] . . . forget you" when he lands in jail!
Psalty also encourages kids to make up songs to help them
remember their verses.

As with all Psalty products, for this new adventure story,
we've chosen struggles and concepts that affect everyone
trying to live their Christian faith. We believe that if you
learn these concepts as a child, they will stay with you
throughout your adult years. And you will be better
equipped to live a joyous life, committed to Christ.

Now snuggle close to your little one and follow Psalty;
his wife, Psaltina; their booklets Rhythm, Melody, and
Harmony; and their trusty dog Blooper on their exciting
adventure to Russia.

Ernie Rettino and Debby Kerner Rettino

PSALTY IN THE SOVIET CIRCUS

Scripture quotations are from the *International Children's Bible, New Century Version*. Copyright © 1983, 1986, 1988 by Word Publishing.

**Library of Congress Cataloging-in-Publication Data**

Rettino, Ernie, 1949-
    Psalty in the Soviet circus / Ernie Rettino and Debby Kerner
Rettino ; design and illustration by Dale Wehlacz.
      p.   cm.
    "Word kids!"
    Summary : Separated from his family on a visit to the Soviet
Union and taken to jail for minor violations. Psalty finds comfort in a
remembered Bible verse.
    ISBN 0-8499-0892-2
    [1. Soviet Union—Fiction.  2. Christian life—Fiction.  3. Books—
Fiction.]  I. Rettino, Debby Kerner, 1951-  .  II. Wehlacz,
Dale, 1960-  ill.  III. Title.
PZ7.R32553Pq   1991
[E]—dc20

                           91-499
                           CIP
                           AC

*Printed in the United States of America*

1 2 3 4 9 RRD 9 8 7 6 5 4 3 2 1

# PSALTY in the Soviet CIRCUS

Characters and Story by
**Ernie Rettino and Debby Kerner Rettino**

Design and Illustration by
**Dale Wehlacz**

**WORD** *Kids!*

WORD PUBLISHING
Dallas·London·Vancouver·Melbourne

The Trans-Siberian Express zoomed down the track toward Moscow. Psalty, his family, and their dog, Blooper, were settled into their cozy room on the train.

"I can't wait to get to Moscow to be in the circus!" said Rhythm.

"Me, neither!" Harmony added.

"Me, neither, too!" barked Blooper.

Once again Psaltina read the telegram inviting them to come to Moscow.

# TELEGRAM

"Dear Psalty and Family:

You are very famous here in the Soviet Union. We have heard that you do acrobatics as a family hobby. Please come and perform for the Moscow Circus. We look forward to meeting you here."

*Sergi*

**Sergi the Ringmaster**

"This is going to be fun!" said Harmony.

"But it's scary going to a new place," added Melody.

"It might feel scary, but we never have to be afraid," comforted Psalty. "The Lord says He will never leave us or forget us. It's right here in my Bible in Hebrews 13:5."

"Let's make up a song with that verse," suggested Harmony. So they did. The music helped them to learn the verse by heart. They might need to remember it sometime.

"It'll be fun to meet new people," Psaltina said.

"Yeah, maybe we'll meet some spies!" Rhythm teased.

The next morning Psalty lifted up his breakfast bagel. Underneath it was this note: "You are being watched."

"All right!" Rhythm breathed out. "There *are* spies!"

"Why would anybody want to spy on us?" said Psalty, as he reached for the butter. Psalty gasped.

"What's wrong, Dear?" Psaltina asked.

"Look at the butter," said Psalty, as though he had seen a spider. There were six pats of butter on the plate, with a word carved on each pat: "Meet in Red Square tomorrow alone."

"It's a spy, Dad. I can feel it in my pages!" said Rhythm with glee.

"There's only one way to solve this," said Psalty. "I'll go to Red Square tomorrow and find out."

The Trans-Siberian Express arrived at the Moscow train station. All the performers from the circus were there to greet them.

"Welcome, Psalty and family," announced Sergi, the ringmaster. "We are glad to have you as our guests."

"Thank you, very much," said Psalty.

"In Russian, *spacebo** means 'thank you.' *Spacebo* for coming," said the ringmaster.

"*Spacebo* for the invitation," returned Psalty.

"Let's go to the circus and practice for the show tomorrow!" said Sergi.

The Russian circus acts were lots of fun for the booklets to watch. There were jugglers, trapeze artists, dancing bears, and lots of funny clowns. When Psalty and his family performed, everyone clapped. No one had ever seen songbooks and a blue and white dog do flips in the air.

After practice the clowns gave Psalty's family a real Russian feast. There was red beet soup called borscht*. Little pancakes, filled with fish and sour cream, were called blini*. There were also fried pastries filled with meat called piroshki*. Lots of delicious desserts were made just in their honor!

They ate so much their pages were about to fall out!

After dinner a little clown named Peter came over to Psalty. He said, "In your country you teach praise songs to kids. Could you teach us some of those songs?"

"I'd love to," said Psalty. They all sang along and had a great time.

"Why don't we teach everyone our *new* song?" suggested Melody.

Psalty opened his Bible. "It's from Hebrews 13:5," he said. "'I will never leave you or forget you.' Making up a song helped us learn the verse by heart."

"I wish I had a Bible of my own like you do," said Peter. "In Russia Bibles are very expensive and hard to find."

Psalty handed his Bible to Peter. "Here, Peter," said Psalty. "I want you to have my Bible as a gift."

"Really? Oh, *spacebo*!" exclaimed Peter.

"Well, it's time to go to the hotel," yawned Psalty. "I'll get the car and bring it to the front of the circus tent."

Psalty was very surprised when he opened the car door. On the dashboard was another mysterious note carved in little pats of butter. It said, "Red Square. Tomorrow. Alone. 1:00 P.M."

Psalty drove up in front of the circus tent and honked the horn. Suddenly two Russian police officers came up to Psalty. "Excuse us," they said. "It is against the law to honk your horn in Moscow except to avoid an accident. May we see your driver's license and passport, please?"

"I'm sorry. I don't have my driver's license or passport with me," answered Psalty. "They must have fallen out of my pages when I was doing flips."

"Hmmm," the police officers said to each other. "What is a big, blue songbook doing honking his horn in Moscow? You look suspicious. Please come with us."

The police officers took Psalty to jail!

"We are going to lock you up until somebody brings your driver's license and passport," one officer said.

"But I have to be in the circus tomorrow. And I have to meet someone in Red Square!" protested Psalty.

Nothing Psalty said could change their minds. They put him in a cell and locked the door. Poor Psalty. He was all alone without his family and without his Bible.

But Psalty remembered his new Bible verse by heart. He sang, "I will never leave you or forget you," and it made him feel much better.

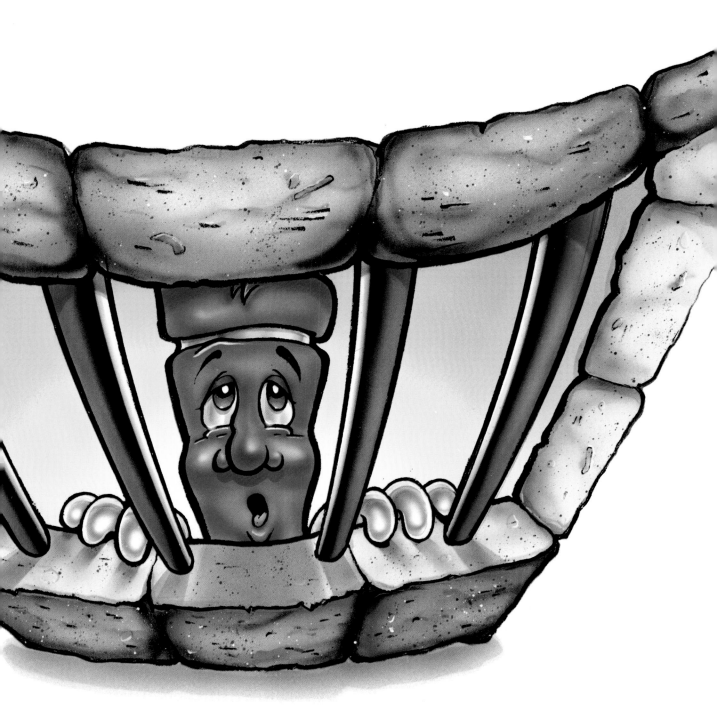

Meanwhile, Psaltina and the booklets, Sergi, and the circus performers looked everywhere for Psalty. They even searched through the cages where the animals slept, but he wasn't there, either.

"Harmony," Rhythm said nervously, "maybe Dad got kidnapped by the . . . spies."

"Uh-oh," said Harmony, "I think it's time to confess. I wrote the note '*You are being watched.*' You were having so much fun, Rhythm, I decided to play a trick on you."

"But what about the butter carvings, '*Meet in Red Square tomorrow alone*'?" asked Melody.

"I bet Dad made those," said Harmony.

"Psaltina!" exclaimed Sergi, "I called the police. Psalty is in jail!"

"In jail!" Psaltina moaned.

"They say to come quickly. All the police are in his cell. Psalty is teaching them praise songs! Let's go!" commanded the ringmaster.

"There he is! Dad! Psalty!" they all yelled at the same time.

"Am I glad to see you!" said a relieved Psalty.

"Do you know this book?" asked the police officer.

"Yes, he is my husband," said Psaltina proudly.

Sergi talked with the police officer. Then Psalty was finally free to go.

"Come back and visit us sometime, Mr. Songbook. You're a lot of fun," said the officers.

"I thought you were taken by spies, Dad," said Rhythm.

"I wrote the first 'spy' note to play a joke on Rhythm," laughed Harmony. "But, Dad, you played a joke on all of us when *you* wrote the second note."

Psalty looked confused, "I didn't write the note."

"You didn't?" said a surprised Melody.

"No, I even found a *third* note in my car reminding me to be in Red Square tomorrow at 1:00 P.M.!" Psalty exclaimed.

"Then it *is* a spy!" Rhythm said excitedly.

The next day at exactly 1:00 P.M., Psalty went to Red Square. Psaltina was there waiting for him!

"Psaltina, it's you!" said Psalty. "I knew all along there was no spy.

"How did you know it was me?" Psaltina asked.

"I'd know your butter carvings anywhere!" laughed Psalty.

"I just wanted a romantic afternoon alone with you," said Psaltina.

Psalty and Psaltina had a wonderful time visiting Red Square all by themselves.

After a week of performing in the Moscow Circus, it was time to go home. All the circus performers came to the train station to say good-bye. Peter, the little clown, gave Psalty a big hug.

"*Spacebo* again for giving me your Bible, Psalty," said Peter. "I will learn it by heart so it is always with me."

"You're welcome, Peter. And *spacebo* to all of you," said Psalty. "We had a wonderful time."

Psalty and his family got on the Trans-Siberian Express. They waved good-bye to all their new friends in the Soviet Union.

They went to their train room and opened the door. There on the table, carved in a big block of butter, was the word *SPACEBO*! Everyone turned and looked at Psaltina who said, "I didn't do it . . . honest!" And they all laughed.

# GLOSSARY

**Spacebo** (spu-cē´-bō) —  A Russian word that means "thank you."

**Borscht** (bôrsht) —  A soup made of beets and cabbage. It often includes potatoes and other vegetables. It may be served with sour cream. And it can be served hot or chilled.

**Blini** (blin´-ē) —  A Russian pancake filled with fish and sour cream.

**Piroshki** (pi-rôsh´-kē) —  A Russian pastry filled with meat or fruit.

**THERE'S MORE TO COME!** Follow Psalty and family's round-the-world adventures in these other great stories:

*PSALTY IN ALASKA*—a snowy dogsled race helps Rhythm learn that we don't have to be afraid of losing if we do our best.

*PSALTY IN THE SOUTH PACIFIC*—being marooned on a South Seas island shows Harmony how trouble can help us grow.

*PSALTY ON SAFARI*—an exciting game-show win and a trip to Africa show Melody that helping with God's work can be more exciting than spending money on herself.

*PSALTY IN EGYPT*—a kidnapping in the shadow of the Great Pyramid ends in a lesson about the life-changing power of prayer and God's love.

*PSALTY IN AUSTRALIA*—a vacation "down under" gives Psalty's family a glimpse of God's amazing creativity and reminds them that God has a unique plan for everyone.